Studies and Melodious Etudes for Bassoon

by

Henry Paine

MW00783812

To The Teacher

"Studies And Melodious Etudes", Level II, is a supplementary technic book of the Belwin "STUDENT INSTRUMENTAL COURSE". Although planned as a companion and correlating book to the method, "The Bassoon Student", it can also be used effectively with most intermediate bassoon instruction books. It provides for extended and additional treatment in technical areas, which are limited in the basic method because of lack of space. Emphasis is on developing musicianship through scales, warm-ups and technical drills, musicianship studies and interesting melody-like etudes.

The Belwin "STUDENT INSTRUMENTAL COURSE" - A course for individual and class instruction of LIKE instruments, at three levels, for all band instruments.

EACH BOOK IS COMPLETE IN ITSELF BUT ALL BOOKS ARE CORRELATED WITH EACH OTHER

METHOD
"The Bassoon Student"

For individual

or

Bassoon class instruction.

ALTHOUGH EACH BOOK CAN BE USED SEPARATELY, IDEALLY, ALL SUPPLEMENTARY BOOKS SHOULD BE USED AS COMPANION BOOKS WITH THE METHOD

STUDIES AND MELODIOUS ETUDES

Supplementary scales, warm-up and technical drills, musicianship studies and melody-like etudes all carefully correlated with the method.

TUNES FOR TECHNIC

Technical type melodies, variations, and "famous passages" from musical literature – for the development of technical dexterity.

BASSOON SOLOS

Four separate correlated solos, with piano accompaniment, written or arranged by Henry Paine:

Spanish Dance No. 2 . . . . *Moszkowski*
Scherzo . . . . *Paine*
Minuet . . . . *Haydn*
Arabesque . . . . *Paine*

Intermediate Fingering Chart

LEFT THUMB

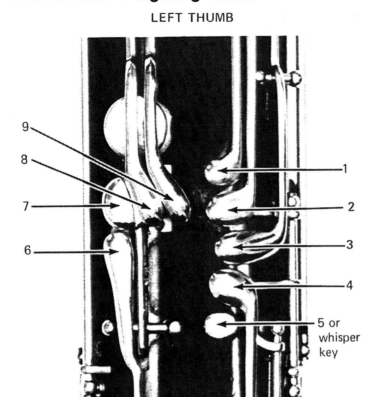

LEFT FINGERS

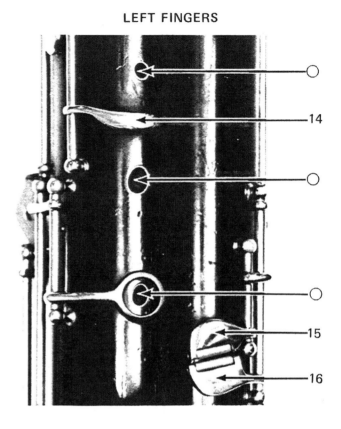

How To Read The Fingering Chart

● — Indicates hole Closed   O— Indicates hole Open.   ⊖ — Indicates hole Half Covered

When a number is given, refer to the pictures for Key numbers.

Key 5 is pressed for ALL NOTES BELOW fourth line F♯.

Will close automatically below low E.

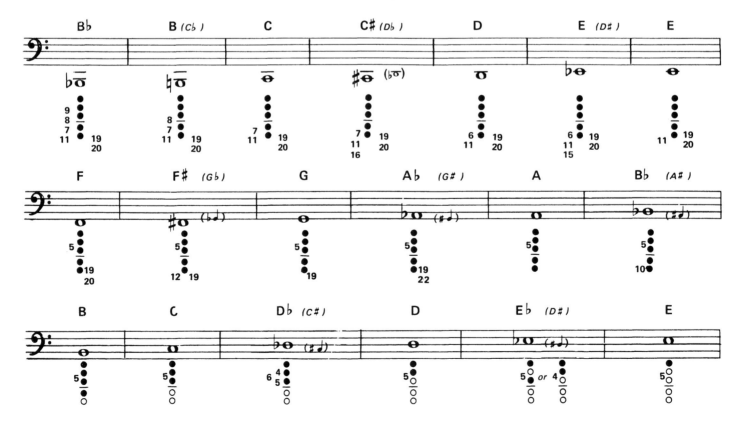

RIGHT THUMB   RIGHT FINGERS

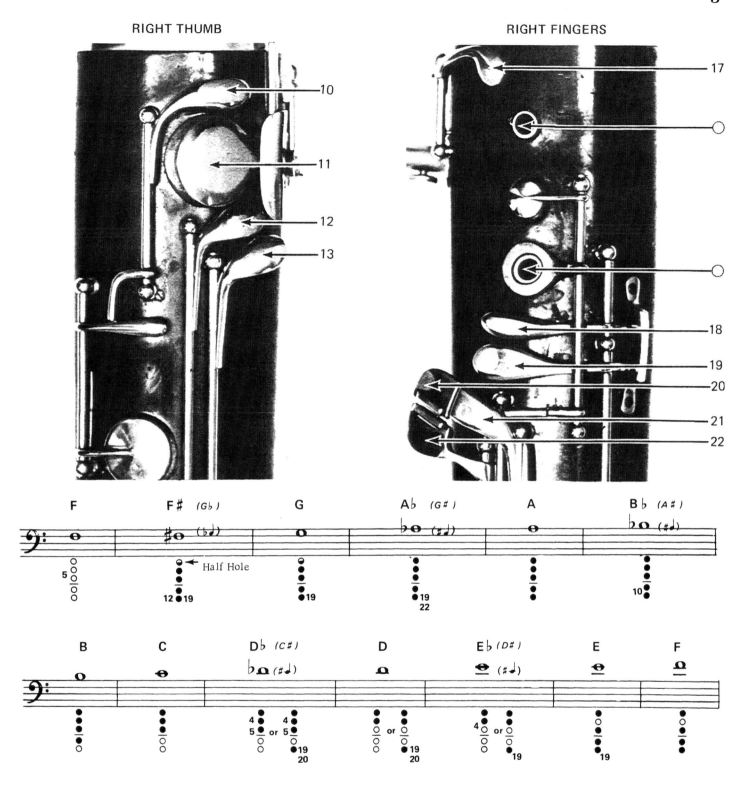

The REED is taken into the mouth with the upper lip almost touching the first wire. *DO NOT PLAY ON THE TIP OF THE REED!* Grasp the reed firmly with the lips being certain that the teeth are NOT in contact with the reed. Draw the chin down and back slightly into an "OVERBITE" position. Keep the lips on the loose side so as not to bite the reed shut. Feel as though you are saying "AH". This will keep the teeth apart and the throat open.

Sit erect and bring the reed into the mouth in a comfortable position. Do not tip the head up, but down only slightly to help the overbite position.

The Studies and Etudes on this page correlate approximately with Page 5, Lesson I of the Bassoon method book "The Bassoon Student", Level II, and the correlation is continued throughout the book.

Etude No. 1

THIRDS

Etude No. 2

g minor scale (Melodic Form)

Etude No. 3

First, tongue all notes — then play as slurred.

Etude No. 4

Andante

f

mf

mp

f

mf

cresc. -   *f*

8

Etude No. 5

Etude No. 6

Slow 6 counts.
(If upper notes are too high, play lower octave.)

Etude No. 7

Also play:

etc.

Etude No. 8

Tonguing exercise practice slowly, then try for speed.

Etude No. 9

Etude No. 10

Allegro

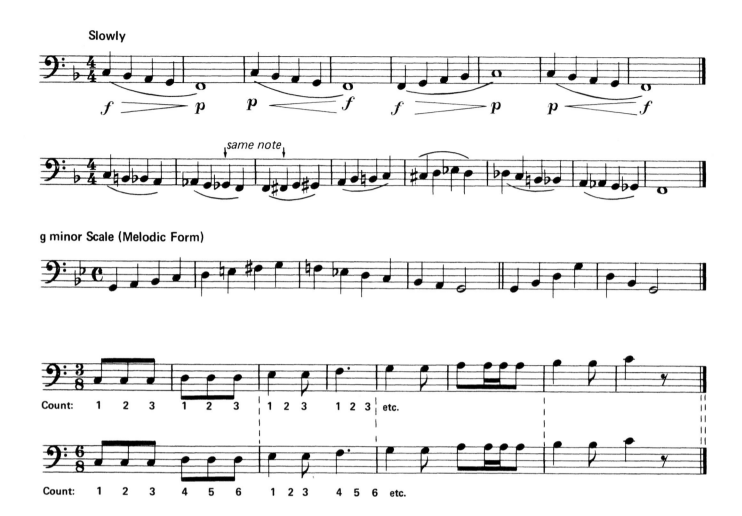

g minor Scale (Melodic Form)

Etude No. 11

Etude No. 12

SYNCOPATED SCALE

Short, detached notes

Also play:

etc.

Count in 6 and 2.

Slow **6/8**   1 2 3 4 5 6   1 2 3   4 5 6   1   2   3   4   5   6   etc.
Fast **6/8**   1   2   1   2   1   2   etc.

Etude No. 13

Play with solid breath

Moderate 2 counts.

sempre stacc.

Count: 1   2   1   2   etc.

Etude No. 14

WEISSENBORN

March - like

f

mf

smoothly

cresc. - *f*   *f*

mf

f

rit. - - - - - - - - - - - - - - - - -

B.I.C.227

18

Etude No. 15

Slowly — then work for speed.

Use various articulations.

Quickly

Etude No. 16

Moderato

f

mf

cresc. - - - - - - - - - - - - - - - - - *f*

mp

mf

f

20

In 2

Lento — means slowly

Lento

Andante

Etude No. 17

Allegretto

mp

cresc.--------

mf

f

mf

mf

f

Etude No. 18

Also play:

Etude No. 19

Play both ways — Work for speed!

Etude No. 20

Also play:

Also play:

Etude No. 21

Practice with various articulations. , etc.

Etude No. 22

Etude No. 23

In slow 2 counts

ARBAN

(F#)

* $\underset{..}{♪}$ = *Divide into two eighth notes.* $\underset{....}{\mathrel{\raise1pt\hbox{$\rlap{—}{\rlap{—}♪}$}}}$ = *Divide into four sixteenth notes.*

Etude No. 24

Etude No. 25

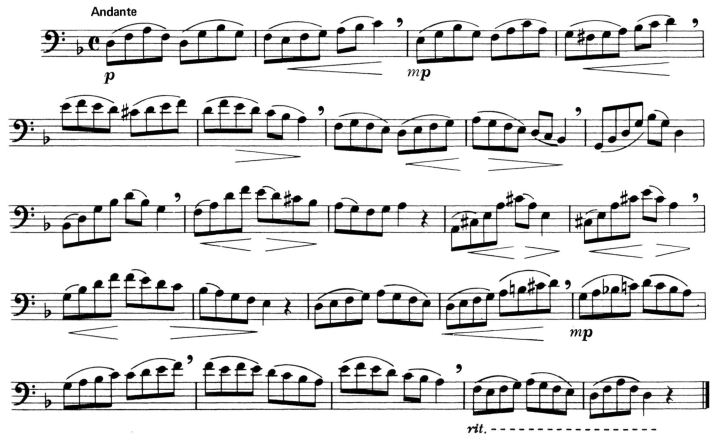

Also play:

etc.

Etude No. 26

Moderato

WEISSENBORN

mf

p

cresc. -

- - - - - - - - f p

f

f

C Major Scale

Octave Study

Andante

mp

Etude No. 27

Andante

WEISSENBORN

f

mf

f

f

mf

mf

cresc. - *f*

Bb Major Scale

Octave study

Andante

Etude No. 28

Moderato

Adapted from KLOSE

32

Commonly Used Major Scales and Their Related Minors.

classic·festival·solos

Volume II

CLASSIC FESTIVAL SOLOS, **Volume II** continues, as in Volume I, to afford the advancing student the opportunity to find performance materials graded from easy to more challenging, including exposure to a variety of musical styles. Many of these works appear on State Contest lists

CLASSIC FESTIVAL SOLOS are available for 16 instruments, each with piano accompaniment. In addition, a book of unaccompanied snare drum solos is offered.

Instrumentation:

C FLUTE
____ (EL03869) **Solo Book**
____ (EL03870) **Piano Accompaniment**

OBOE
____ (EL03871) **Solo Book**
____ (EL03872) **Piano Accompaniment**

B♭ CLARINET
____ (EL03873) **Solo Book**
____ (EL03874) **Piano Accompaniment**

E♭ ALTO CLARINET
____ (EL03875) **Solo Book**
____ (EL03876) **Piano Accompaniment**

B♭ BASS CLARINET
____ (EL03877) **Solo Book**
____ (EL03878) **Piano Accompaniment**

BASSOON
____ (EL03879) **Solo Book**
____ (EL03880) **Piano Accompaniment**

E♭ ALTO SAXOPHONE
____ (EL03881) **Solo Book**
____ (EL03882) **Piano Accompaniment**

B♭ TENOR SAXOPHONE
____ (EL03883) **Solo Book**
____ (EL03884) **Piano Accompaniment**

E♭ BARITONE SAXOPHONE
____ (EL03885) **Solo Book**
____ (EL03886) **Piano Accompaniment**

B♭ TRUMPET
____ (EL03887) **Solo Book**
____ (EL03888) **Piano Accompaniment**

HORN IN F
____ (EL03889) **Solo Book**
____ (EL03890) **Piano Accompaniment**

TROMBONE
____ (EL03891) **Solo Book**
____ (EL03892) **Piano Accompaniment**

BARITONE (Bass Clef)
____ (EL03893) **Solo Book**
____ (EL03894) **Piano Accompaniment**

TUBA
____ (EL03895) **Solo Book**
____ (EL03896) **Piano Accompaniment**

MALLET PERCUSSION
____ (EL03897) **Solo Book**
____ (EL03898) **Piano Accompaniment**

SNARE DRUM
____ (EL03899) **Solo Book**
____ (EL03900) **Piano Accompaniment**

SNARE DRUM
____ (EL03901) **Solo Book (Unaccompanied)**

Belwin

Alfred

alfred.com

ISBN-10: 0-7579-1673-2
ISBN-13: 978-0-7579-1673-1

BIC00227A $6.95 in USA

ISBN 0-7579-1673-2

Festive Strings

For String Quartet or String Orchestra
Arranged and Edited by Joanne Martin

SUMMY-BIRCHARD INC.

Alfred